THE WORLD OF

PETER RABBIT™

The Christmas present Hunt

Based on the books by

BEATRIX POTTER

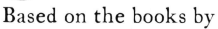

Peter Rabbit was **SO** excited for Christmas.

He had helped his mum make mince pies and sung Christmas carols at the top of his voice.

Soon, it would be time
for the best job of all . . .

Putting the
presents under the tree!

Peter had made his mother and sisters a
present each, carefully wrapped in brown paper.
He had hidden them in his **secret** hiding place,
where he always kept **important things.**

But when he went to move
the presents from his secret
hiding place . . .

. . . they weren't there!

Oh no! Where had they gone?

Then Peter remembered! He'd had to move them when he was playing hide and seek with his sisters. Under his bed was always Cotton-tail's favourite place to hide.

The little rabbit headed out to look for them, trying to remember where he had put them all.

But so much snow had fallen that the forest looked so **different** from before. Peter was quickly confused, but he had to find the presents before it was time for bed!

First, Peter looked
in the snowy forest.

Perhaps he had
hidden one there?

As he looked, his cousin appeared. Benjamin was **very** good at finding things and offered to help.

But who would be the **first** to find them?

One present found!
Peter carefully put it in his basket and tried to remember where the others could be . . .

"Did you give them to someone to look after?" asked Benjamin. "Mr. Jeremy Fisher perhaps? He is very careful, I would trust him to look after a present."

That's right! Peter had given Mopsy's present to Mr. Fisher to look after – he knew where to go next.

"Ah, yes, I put your sister's present in a very **safe place** along with some holly decorations," said Jeremy Fisher. "But where was that?"

Mr. Jeremy Fisher and the bunnies began to look all about the pond. They had to be careful not to **slip** on the ice!

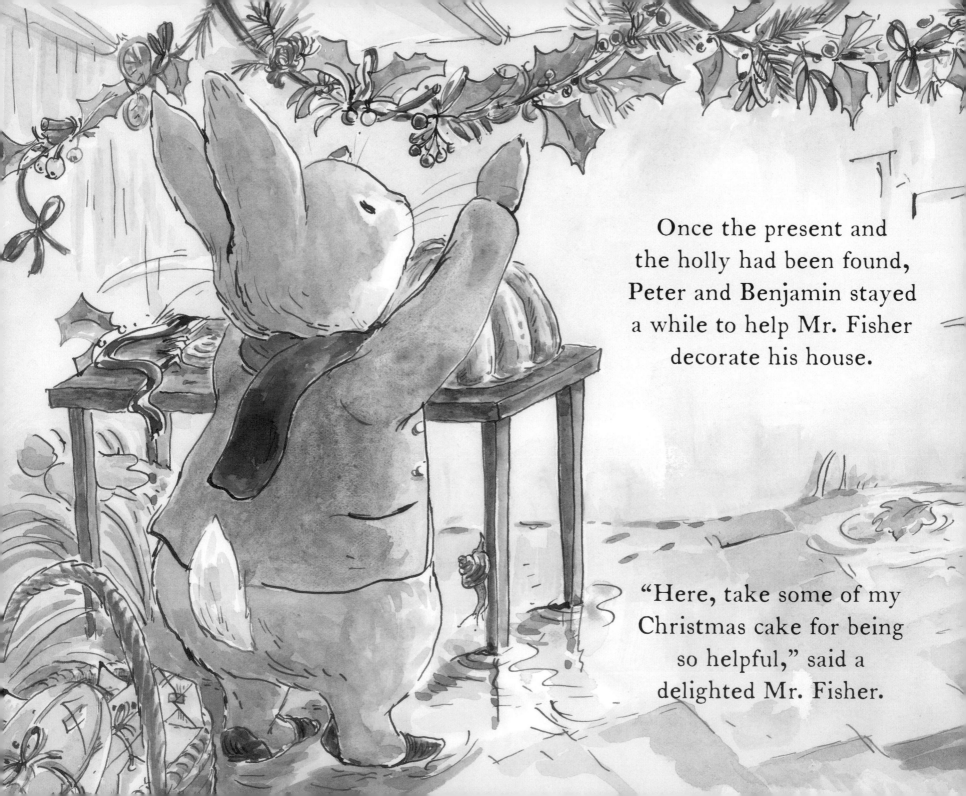

Once the present and the holly had been found, Peter and Benjamin stayed a while to help Mr. Fisher decorate his house.

"Here, take some of my Christmas cake for being so helpful," said a delighted Mr. Fisher.

As the rabbits stepped outside, Mr. Fisher called, "Oh, and Peter, I think you may want to try the farm next. I'm sure I saw you there with a present not so long ago."

The cousins happily nibbled on the cake, dropping a trail of crumbs, as they looked around the farmyard.

Jemima was singing Christmas songs with her ducklings. They were even **more excited** than Peter!

Now Peter just had his
mother's present to find.
Where could it be?

"Perhaps more cake will help you remember," suggested Benjamin. Peter quickly agreed. The cake was **rather** tasty.

The kind little bunnies shared their cake with the ducklings and everyone in the barn began to sing again.

The animals were having such a good time that they didn't notice the sun had started to set.

Peter and Benjamin jumped up and rushed off with their basket.

They still had to find Mrs. Rabbit's present before Christmas Day came!

They looked **everywhere** on their way home but they had no luck at all. Peter was very sad as he waved goodbye to Benjamin.

What was a little rabbit to do?

But then Peter
spotted something
sparkly behind a snowy
tree trunk . . .

Peter was **SO** pleased!
He carefully placed each
present under the tree,
ready for his family
to open.

Mrs. Rabbit smiled as she placed some
of her **tastiest** mince pies, a carrot
and a glass of milk on a plate
for Father Christmas.

Her sleepy bunnies were
all asleep and dreaming
of the festive fun
tomorrow would bring.